This Walker book belongs to

....

....

....

To Daniel,
S.M^cB.

For Steve,
A.J.

First published 2007 by Walker Books Ltd
87 Vauxhall Walk, London SE11 5HJ

This edition published 2016

10 9 8 7 6 5 4 3 2 1

Text © 1994 – 2016 Sam McBratney
Illustrations © 1994 – 2016 Anita Jeram

Guess How Much I Love You™ is
a trademark of Walker Books Ltd, London.

The right of Sam McBratney and Anita Jeram to be
identified as author and illustrator respectively of this
work has been asserted by them in accordance with
the Copyright, Designs and Patents Act 1988.

This book has been typeset in Cochin.

Printed and bound in China.

British Library Cataloguing in
Publication Data: a catalogue record
for this book is available from the
British Library.

ISBN 978-1-4063-7231-1

www.guesshowmuchiloveyou.com
www.walker.co.uk

GUESS HOW MUCH I LOVE YOU

——— *in the* ———

WINTER

Written by

Sam McBratney

Illustrated by

Anita Jeram

WALKER BOOKS

AND SUBSIDIARIES

LONDON • BOSTON • SYDNEY • AUCKLAND

Little Nutbrown Hare
and Big Nutbrown Hare went
out in the winter snow.

They played I Spy as they
hopped through the snow.
Little Nutbrown Hare
looked around until he
saw something interesting.

"I spy something that belongs
to a tree," he said.

Big Nutbrown Hare
did some thinking
about trees.

"Could it be a leaf?"

It was the right answer!

Now it was Big Nutbrown
Hare's turn to look around him.

"I spy something that
belongs to a spider."

"A web!" said
Little Nutbrown Hare.

Yes! A web was the answer.

"I spy something that
belongs to a bird," said
Little Nutbrown
Hare.

Big Nutbrown
Hare thought
about birds
for a while.

Then he said, "Could it be a feather?"

Yes! It was a feather.

"This time," said
Big Nutbrown Hare, "I spy something that
belongs to the river. And it's wet, wet, wet."

"Water!" cried Little Nutbrown Hare.

Water was the answer.

Little Nutbrown Hare began to laugh.
I've got a good one, he thought.
"I spy something that belongs to me."

Big Nutbrown Hare was puzzled.
"Can I have a clue?" he said.

"It's only there when the
sun comes out."

"Your shadow!" said
Big Nutbrown
Hare.

Then Big Nutbrown Hare said,

"I spy something that belongs to *me*
and it's not my shadow."

This was a really tricky one.
Little Nutbrown Hare did some
thinking, and then he said,

"Can I have a clue?"

"It's little... It's nutbrown...
It's my most favourite thing...

And it can hop."

"Me!"

Other *Guess How Much I Love You* Books

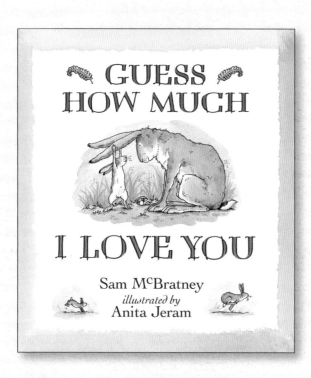

With more than 35 million copies sold, *Guess How Much I Love You* is one of the world's best-loved picture books.

The endearing simplicity of Sam McBratney's story and Anita Jeram's exquisite watercolours make it a modern classic.

ISBN 978-1-4063-0040-6

Available now

ISBN 978-1-4063-5743-1

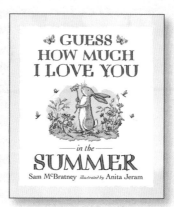

ISBN 978-1-4063-5817-9

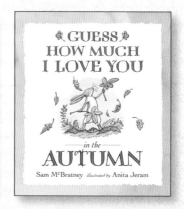

ISBN 978-1-4063-5970-1

Coming soon to all good booksellers

www.walker.co.uk